A Wild Weather Day

by Judith Stamper
Illustrated by Duendes Del Sur

SCHOLASTIC INC.
New York   Toronto   London   Auckland   Sydney
Mexico City   New Delhi   Hong Kong

Chapter 1

It was a wild and windy day.
The JumpStart ship was headed
for Tree Fort Island.

Frankie was at the wheel.
The sails flapped in the wind.
The ship raced through the water.

"Why are we going so fast?"
Pierre asked.
"The wind is blowing us along on our
adventure," CJ said. "Did you know that
wind is just air that is strong and fast?"
"Like Frankie!" Pierre said. "He's strong and
fast, too."

"Why is the sky getting so dark?" Pierre asked.

"I know why it's dark!" Eleanor said.
"Clouds get dark when they fill up
with tiny drops of water."
"Look — they're almost the same color
as your bow," Pierre said.

SPLAT! A big drop of rain fell on Pierre's nose.
"Oh, no!" he said. "It's starting to rain!"

"The rain is coming from the clouds," CJ said.
"The water in the clouds got too heavy, and now
it's falling down on us!"
"Just like when Hopsalot waters his garden,"
said Pierre.

Chapter 2

The ship reached Tree Fort Island
just in time!
The rain began to pour from the sky.
The gang ran for the clubhouse.

DRIP! DROP! PLIP! PLOP!
Big raindrops smacked against the windows.
SPLIT! SPLAT! SPLIT!
Rain pounded on the roof.

"I don't like rain!" Pierre cried out.
"But rain is good!" Eleanor said.
"Everything needs rain to live.
Plants need rain. Animals need rain.
Without rain, we'd all dry up!"

ZAP! A big flash of lightning lit up the sky.
"Oooh!" Pierre said. "What's that flash of light?"

"That's lightning — it's like a giant spark of electricity. It's shooting down from a cloud to the ground," Frankie said. "But don't worry! We're safe inside."

"We're warm inside, too," said Pierre.

BOOM! A loud clap of thunder shook the
clubhouse.

Pierre and Eleanor looked out the window.

"Where does that scary sound come from?"
asked Pierre.

"Thunder comes from the lightning," Eleanor
said. "The air heats up so fast that it booms!"

"Just like a giant drum!" said Pierre.

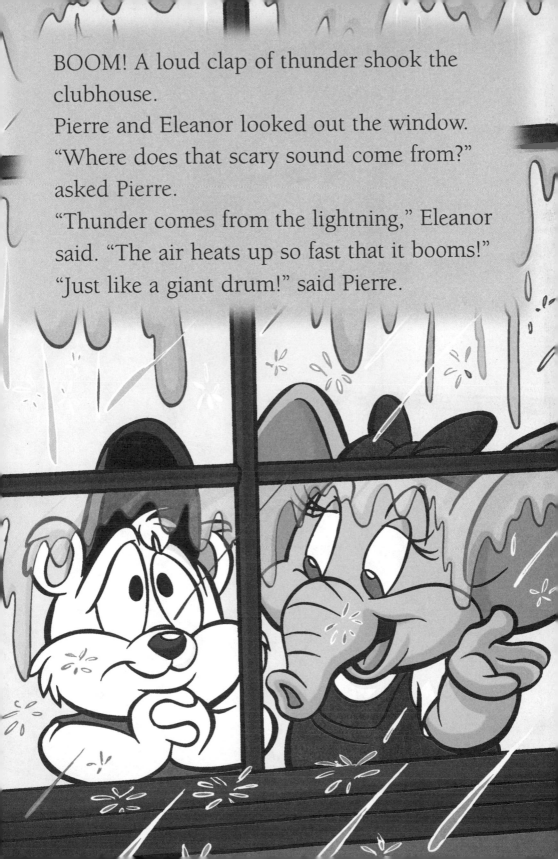

"Jumping gerbils! It's hail!" Hopsalot said. "The water in the air got really cold. The raindrops turned into balls of ice. When they fall from the sky, that's called hail!"

"They're like ice cubes that come from the sky!" Pierre said.

Chapter 3

Outside, the storm raged and roared. Inside, everyone had fun drinking cocoa and eating snacks.

"I'm not so afraid anymore," Pierre said.

Then the sky went from dark to light.
The wind stopped blowing.
The rain stopped falling.
The lightning and thunder went away.

"I wonder if there will
be a rainbow," Kisha said.
"Let's find out," Frankie said.
The whole gang ran outside.

"There it is," Eleanor said. "A rainbow!"
"Look at those pretty colors," Kisha said.
"The sun shines through the raindrops
and makes the colors appear."

"Storms go away," Pierre said to Frankie.
"But friends are here to stay."